L E G E N D S
Battles and Quests

LEGENDS

ANTHONY HOROWITZ

Battles and Quests

Illustrated by Thomas Yeates

KINGFISHER
NEW YORK

KINGFISHER
LONDON & NEW YORK

First American hardback edition published 2010 by Kingfisher
First American paperback edition published 2011 by Kingfisher

Distributed in the U.S. by Macmillan,
175 Fifth Ave., New York, NY 10010
Distributed in Canada by H.B. Fenn and Company Ltd.,
34 Nixon Road, Bolton, Ontario L7E 1W2

Library of Congress Cataloging-in-Publication data
has been applied for.

ISBN: 978-0-7534-6632-2

Kingfisher books are available for special promotions and
premiums. For details contact: Special Markets Department,
Macmillan, 175 Fifth Ave., New York, NY 10010.

For more information, please visit
www.kingfisherbooks.com

Printed and bound in the U.K. by
CPI Mackays, Chatham ME5 8TD
1 3 5 7 9 8 6 4 2

Contents

Introduction

This introduction is shorter than the introduction that you'll find in my other book of myths and legends: *Beasts and Monsters*, but it actually says much the same thing. I just think it's important to explain that this is not a new book.

In fact, I wrote most of these stories a very long time ago, when I was twenty-eight. They were published in a book called *The Kingfisher Book of Myths and Legends*, which means that one way or another they have been in print for almost thirty years.

I would never have gone back to them, but a couple of rather pleasant editors from Macmillan (who had taken over Kingfisher) came to see me with an idea. Rummaging through the Kingfisher filing cabinets, they had come across my old manuscripts and wondered if I would be interested in republishing them. They said they would provide new, improved illustrations and better covers. Even the glue that held the books together, they promised me, would be superior.

I happily agreed to the idea. But then it seemed only reasonable that I should take a look at the stories myself and do a bit of tidying up. It was quite interesting reading what I'd written all those years ago—a bit like meeting myself in a time warp. Anyway, I shortened a couple of the stories and rearranged some of the others. There were one or two boring bits which I cut. I also took out some of the more stupid jokes.

But the basic idea remains the same. To tell these stories as if for the first time.

I've always loved myths and legends. You have to think about ancient people in caves, looking out at a world that they couldn't possibly understand. Where did the sun go at night? Where did the stars come from? What made the wind blow? Trying to answer these questions, they invented gods and goddesses, heroes and monsters. And just telling the stories must have brought them together and made them feel safe.

The stories that are most familiar to us tend to come from ancient Greece. Theseus and the

Minotaur, for example, is by far the best known story in this collection. But I really wanted to travel a little further, and so you'll also find some rather more obscure myths and legends which you may not have heard before, including one from the Bororo Indians of South America. These stories may feel very strange, but I suppose they do tell us something about the people who invented them. And that's something else to remember. I've tried to make the stories feel modern by adding a bit of color and description as well as a few extra thoughts of my own, but I haven't changed the basic narrative.

Anyway, that's enough introduction. Who reads it anyway? If all goes well, there will be two more books next year and two more the year after that. It reminds me that I won't be around forever. But on the other hand, these stories probably will.

Anthony Horowitz

The Minotaur

Greek

The Minotaur

There was a time when Athens was not the major city that it is today, but a small town perched on the edge of a cliff some three miles from the sea. King Aegeus was on the throne and he was a good ruler. There were no wars, there was plenty of food to go around, and no plagues or monsters inhabited the land.

And yet, once every seven years, something strange would happen. There would be no alarm, no signal, but suddenly the streets would empty. Men and women would hurry home, avoiding each other's eyes, gathering up their children and taking them indoors. It would seem as if Athens had been deserted. And inside their homes, families would sit together, hiding in the shadows, and nobody would speak.

A stranger, walking through the town, might think that some terrible catastrophe had just occurred. And yet there would be no sign of any damage, like that caused by an earthquake or a fire. The streets would be clean and orderly, even if all the shops were closed for business. Trees carrying the first spring blossoms would surround him if he strolled into the parks.

A mystery.

Standing there, the stranger might feel a cold wind whisper through the streets and, if he listened carefully, he might just be able to hear what it was saying.

The Minotaur

"Minos is coming. Minos will soon be here . . . "

And hearing that, he would understand. He would turn and hurry out of this accursed place, leaving the wretched people to their fate. Throughout ancient Greece everyone knew what had happened to the son of King Minos and the cruel revenge that he had demanded. They also knew the terrible secret that lay hidden deep underneath his palace.

The Minotaur.

But even the breeze was too afraid to speak that name. It would rush through the streets saying nothing more, twisting around the corners as if it too was in a hurry to get away.

The Birth of the Minotaur

Minos was the king of Crete, the Island of the Hundred Cities. He was one of the most powerful sovereigns in the world and his

5

island was one of the most magnificent. Its harbor was huge, built to hold a hundred ships and surrounded by towering walls and guarded by turrets that were manned twenty-four hours a day. The capital—Knossos—was a mass of color and life. The Cretan people, all too aware of their status, loved to wear expensive clothes and to eat the most luxurious food, brought to them from the farthest corners of the civilized world. The market stalls, jammed together in the narrow streets, were always piled high with the finest goods, including silks and satins, exotic spices, ivory and jewels, rare parrots, performing monkeys, and much, much more. While the sun shone, the buying and selling never stopped, and even at night, once the torches had been lit, dancers and fire-eaters, snake charmers and magicians would come out to entertain the crowds.

And yet there was a darker side to Crete. And even Minos, for all his wealth and success, could not escape from its shadow.

The Minotaur. It was like a cancer beneath the skin, the unpleasant truth that spoils everything that is exposed to it. Minos would have gladly emptied the markets and thrown all the riches into the sea if he could have gotten rid of it. And the worst of it was—it was all his fault. If it hadn't been for his own greed and stupidity, the Minotaur would never have existed. He had made one mistake. He had been paying for it ever since.

This is how it had happened.

Every year, for many years, Minos had sacrificed the best bull from his herd to Poseidon. Crete depended on its sea power and Poseidon was, of course, the god of the sea. One year, however, acting in a moment of madness, Minos had decided to hold back his best animal . . . a huge white bull, the likes of which he had never seen before. From such a beast he could breed a whole herd of prize cattle. It would be a complete

waste to slaughter it and then burn its remains on an altar. Surely Poseidon wouldn't notice if he sacrificed another, slightly less magnificent bull in its place.

That was what Minos thought, but of course Poseidon did notice and his anger was as terrible as his revenge was strange and cruel. He left Minos untouched but turned his powers on the king's wife, the young and innocent Queen Pasiphaë, making her fall in love with the white bull. Not knowing what she was doing, the queen stole away one stormy night to the stables and it was from this unnatural union that the Minotaur was born.

Minotaur means, simply, "Minos bull."

King Minos and his wife looked after the ugly creature for as long as they could, trying to keep it away from prying eyes. But the moment it was strong enough to walk, the Minotaur broke free and left the palace. In the days that followed, it went berserk, destroying much of Crete and killing many of its inhabitants. It was as if a psychopathic murderer had arrived on the island. It didn't kill for any other reason than because it had to.

Minos was filled with shame and horror. In desperation, he turned to the oracle to find out what to do. He couldn't kill the creature. It was, after all, his wife's child.

But how could he deal with it? How could he avoid the terrible scandal that now surrounded him?

As usual, the oracle had all the answers. She told the king to build a labyrinth at Knossos in which to conceal both the Minotaur and his own unfortunate wife. The maze would be so complicated, with so many twists and turns, so many false starts and dead ends, that no man, once trapped inside it, would find his way out. The two of them could remain there, safe and secure. Minos would never see either of them again.

Minos did what the oracle had suggested. He commissioned his court architect, a man called Daedalus, to do the work—and the maze was so fantastic that several of the slaves who built it disappeared without a trace. And that might have been the end of it. Minos might have continued his rule, alone and lonely, but a little wiser about how to deal with the gods.

However, a few months later, another event took place that was once more going to change his life. Minos had a son whom he loved, a boy called Androgeus. Shortly after the Minotaur had been incarcerated, Androgeus set sail for the town of Athens to take part in the Pan-Athenian games, which were held there every five years. He was a strong, skillful athlete and he did well, winning several of the events outright. Soon he found himself being cheered on as the

favorite of the crowd, much to the resentment of the royal court and in particular the nephews of King Aegeus.

These nephews were an unpleasant bunch who spent their time fighting in the streets and lounging around the palace. Now, envious of the success of Androgeus, they lay in ambush one evening after the games had ended and fell on him as he walked home to his lodgings. Androgeus fought bravely but he was heavily outnumbered. The gang killed him and left his body in the road.

When Minos heard of this he was beside himself with grief and rage. At once he ordered his fleet to set sail, and the next day, when King Aegeus awoke, he found the town surrounded. Fighting was impossible. The Cretan army completely encircled the town, and the fleet itself, anchored in the shallows just off the coast, was larger than the whole of Athens. Aegeus had no choice. Kneeling before Minos, he surrendered himself and his town to the Cretan king's mercy.

"I come in search of my son's assassins," Minos said. "Yield them to me and I will leave you unharmed."

"I can't do that," King Aegeus replied. "I'm sorry, great king. It was a miserable deed and I would gladly give you the killers if I knew who they were. But I don't! The cowards remain hidden. And so we must all suffer for their crime."

"And suffer you will," Minos said. He thought for a moment, then came to a terrible decision. "This is my decree," he continued. "I have lost a son. The sons and the daughters of Athens will have to pay the price. At the end of every Great Year, which is to say, every seven years, you will send me your seven bravest young men and your seven most beautiful maidens. Do not ask what will happen to them! All that matters is that you will never see them again.

"This will be your tribute to me for the death of my eldest child. Fail, and Athens will burn."

The Minotaur

There was nothing King Aegeus could do. Every seven years, the fourteen Athenians were chosen by lottery and taken away by ship to Crete and an unknown death. And in Crete, while the colorful throng jostled in the streets, the Minotaur stalked its victims through the subterranean maze and killed them to satisfy its lust for blood.

The Coming of Theseus

Nobody would ever forget the day that Theseus entered Athens. The fact that he had arrived at all was considered remarkable because he had chosen to take the coastal road, which was a home to all manner of thieves and bandits. Few travelers came that way—but not only had Theseus been unharmed, he had managed to kill no fewer than five of the worst offenders, kicking one of them over a cliff, lopping off the legs of another, and crushing a third with a huge boulder.

Theseus was actually the son of King Aegeus although the two of them had never met—for Aegeus had left Theseus's mother before the boy was born. In any event, Aegeus was delighted to see him. Theseus was seventeen years old. He was strong, fearless, good-looking, and intelligent . . . in short everything a man could have hoped for in a son. Aegus's nephews, unfortunately, were less amused. Once again, they became envious and decided to give him exactly the same treatment as poor Androgeus. It was a big mistake. Theseus killed every single one of them and the fact that they were, technically, his cousins didn't bother him a bit.

Aegeus was actually delighted by this turn of events. His nephews had been getting more and more out of hand and he had even been afraid they might one day turn on him. So that night there was a celebration such as Athens had never seen before. Great bonfires were lit and oxen sacrificed

The Minotaur

to the gods. It seemed that in every street tables and chairs were laid out for a banquet that stretched its way around the entire town. There was dancing and fireworks, and at midnight Aegeus stood up to announce that from now on Theseus would be known as the Prince of Athens and that one day he would inherit the throne. The stars were brilliant that night and, for a short while, Crete and the Minotaur were forgotten.

But time would not stand still and, inevitably, the end of another Great Year approached. Once again, the shadow returned. With the coming of spring the old disease reappeared in the streets, that terrible fear of unspoken things. And one day, when the blossoms were at their most beautiful, the ship from the Cretan court arrived at the coast to collect the tribute of seven men and seven women.

"The Minotaur . . ."

Theseus had never even heard of the tribute that King Minos had demanded, and he begged his father to tell him what was happening. Reluctantly, Aegeus explained what had happened twenty-one years before— for this was the third time that the ship with the black sails had come to Athens.

"It's not fair!" Theseus cried. "Didn't I kill the murderers of Androgeus with my own hands? We have paid the tribute in full. Enough is enough!"

"King Minos still demands the tribute," Aegeus said.

"I won't allow it!"

"You can't prevent it. We must pay the tribute until the Minotaur is destroyed, and that will never happen, for its victims are fed to it without weapons, without any hope of survival."

"And what does this monster look like?" Theseus asked.

"Nobody has ever lived to describe it."

"Then I will have to find out for myself. I will travel as one of the seven men and I will enter the creature's cave and destroy it. Then, perhaps, Minos will be content."

Aegeus tried to dissuade him, but Theseus wouldn't listen. The unfortunate fourteen had already been chosen and were about to be led to the port but at the last moment he arranged for one of the men and two of the women to be freed.

"I'll take the man's place," he explained. "And two soldiers will come with me. They can put on dresses and make-up and come as girls. King Minos won't be expecting anything and with a little luck no one will look too closely."

King Aegeus was still unhappy about all this—but now he gave Theseus a white sail. "I am an old man," he said. "Perhaps there are not many days left to me. So should you succeed in this perilous quest, journey home with this white sail on your mast. That way I will know all the sooner that my beloved son is safe."

But it was with black sails that they departed from Athens, carried by the southerly wind to Crete. It took them just two days to reach the island, where a huge crowd was waiting for them in the harbor. Minos himself was there to count the victims, to check that Aegeus had not tried to cheat him and to cast an eye over the maidens to see if any were worthy of the royal bed.

He did indeed see such a girl (fortunately not one of the soldiers in disguise) and gave orders for her to be taken to the palace. But as the palace guards stepped forward, Theseus suddenly leaped between them.

"Is this how the tyrant of Crete greets his guests?" he shouted so that all could hear. "Is this the sort of behavior we can expect from a great king?"

At this, Minos trembled with anger. "And who do you think you are, boy?" he snarled.

"I am Theseus, Prince of Athens. The god of the sea, Poseidon, is my protector. And I'm not afraid of you, King Minos."

It was true that Poseidon had always looked kindly on Theseus. The god had been fond of his mother and had once promised her that he would look on her firstborn child as his own.

However, when Minos heard this, he just

laughed. "Poseidon!" he exclaimed. "It's easy enough for arrogant young princes to claim kinship with the gods. But let's see you prove it." He took off a heavy gold signet ring that he had been wearing and cast it into the sea. "If Poseidon is your friend, ask him to bring back the ring for me."

Minos laughed again, and this time his laughter was taken up by the crowd until the whole harbor was filled with the sound of it. Theseus stood alone, pale and defiant, while his thirteen fellow Athenians waited nervously to see what would happen.

Then, suddenly, there was a loud splashing in the harbor and a silver dolphin sprang out of the water, soared high into the air, then twisted and dived down again. As the laughter faded away, the dolphin leaped up a second time, this time actually flying in a great arc over the boat. As it went, something gold dropped from its mouth and landed at the feet of Theseus. He leaned down and picked it up. It was the king's ring.

The laughter quickly died away.

"So it seems that you are who you say you are," Minos growled. "The more's the pity, Theseus. For you have come here as part of my tribute and tomorrow you must die." He turned his back on the Athenian ship. "Take them to the palace," he snapped.

All this had been watched by a young girl who had been sitting by the king, holding herself back only with difficulty. Her eyes had been fixed on Theseus from the moment he had arrived. Minos had risen up and was already walking back to the palace, but as she followed him she turned back to look once again at the prince. "Theseus . . ." She made no sound, but her lips formed the word. And as she went, she smiled to herself.

The Slaying of the Minotaur

She came to him that night, slipping past the guards and using a duplicate key to gain entrance to his cell.

"Theseus," she whispered, once the door was safely locked behind her. "My name is Ariadne. I am the daughter of King Minos . . ."

"Then you are no friend of mine," Theseus said.

"But I want to be! I want to be more than your friend." She ran her eyes hungrily over his body. Theseus had been about to sleep and he was naked from the waist up. "If you will take me . . . as your wife, I will help you kill my half-brother, the Minotaur."

"You can help?"

"Of course." She stroked his arm with her hand, marveling at the firmness of his muscles. "I can take you there now. And see—I have a sword."

"But they tell me there is a labyrinth . . ."

"You have nothing to fear." Her lips were so close to his ear that he could feel the warmth of her breath. One of her fingers was curling and uncurling a lock of his dark hair. "I will give you a ball of thread," she continued. "Tie one end to the entrance and unwind it as you go in and you'll have no trouble finding your way out. But remember what you've promised me. I want to be married to you. I want you to be mine."

"Lady," Theseus said, pulling himself away from her distastefully. Then he remembered that she was actually helping him and tried to smile. "If I succeed in killing the Minotaur, then I will certainly do what you ask."

Ariadne nodded. Theseus took the sword and followed her through the sleeping palace, dodging into the shadows whenever a guard appeared. He had been locked in a room on the ground floor and now they descended two stairways, heading deep into the ground below the palace. There were no windows. Their path was lit by low-burning lamps. At the bottom there was a bare corridor leading to a heavy wooden door. Ariadne gave him the ball of thread, tying one end to the handle.

"This is where the labyrinth begins, my love," she said. "I must leave you here. Be quick! Be safe!"

Theseus nodded but said nothing. He was beginning to think that between Ariadne and the Minotaur there wasn't a lot to choose.

He opened the door and stepped through.

It was cold on the other side. Theseus was in a subterranean world, where the sun had never shone and a damp chill hung in the air. The walls were built with huge stone blocks and even three paces away from the door the corridor branched out in a dozen

different directions. Unrolling the ball of thread, Theseus tiptoed forward. There were no lights, but some freak property of the rock had filled the caverns with a ghostly green glow.

Theseus clasped his sword more tightly and continued forward. Despite himself, he could not help but admire the cunning of Daedalus. But for the lifeline that connected him with the exit, he would already have been hopelessly lost. He turned left and then right half a dozen times, noticing that he had somehow crossed his own path, for he could see the thread snaking along the ground ahead of him.

"Where are you?" he whispered to himself. His breath formed a phosphorescent cloud in front of his mouth. The air smelled of seaweed. He shivered and went on, no longer caring which direction he took.

Every direction looked the same. Every corner he turned took him nowhere. Every archway he chose led only into another identical passage. Kicking something loose with his foot, he glanced down.

A human skull rolled against the wall and lay still. He swallowed hard. The immense silence of the labyrinth seemed to bear down on him.

"Where are you?" he said again, more loudly this time. The words scuttled down the corridors, rebounding off the walls.

"Where are you . . . where are you . . . are you . . . ?"

Something stirred.

He heard its breathing, then the scrape of feet on sand. The breathing was slow, irregular, like an animal in pain. He turned another corner and found himself in an open arena, surrounded by archways. Was this where the sound had come from? He could see nothing. No. There it was again. He spun around. A bulky figure stood in one of the archways. It grunted. Then it moved toward him.

The Minotaur was horrible, far more

horrible than he could ever have imagined. It was about the size of a man, but a very large one. Stark naked it stood before him, its fists clenched, its legs slightly apart. The creature was filthy—with dirt and dried blood. A blue moss clung to one side of its body like rust. Despite the chill, sweat dripped from its shoulders, glistening on its skin.

It was human as far up as the neck. Its head was that of a bull . . . and it was grotesquely disproportionate to the rest of its body. So heavy was the head that its human neck was straining to support it, a pulse thudding next to its throat. Two horns curved into the air above a pair of orange eyes. Saliva frothed around its muzzle and splashed onto the stone floor. Its teeth were not those of a bull but of a lion, jutting out of its mouth and gnashing constantly as if the creature were trying to make them fit more comfortably. It carried a piece of twisted iron, holding it like a club.

Theseus stood where he was in the center of the arena while the Minotaur approached him. He didn't move as it raised its clumsy weapon. Only at the last moment, as the iron bar whistled down toward his head, did he raise his own sword. There was a deafening clash as metal struck metal. The Minotaur reeled away, bellowing with surprise, for none of its victims had ever carried a weapon. Taking advantage of the surprise, Theseus lashed forward, but the Minotaur was too fast. It twisted away, receiving nothing worse than a gash on one arm. Then it put

its head
down
and
charged.
Many
young men
and women
had ended
their lives
impaled on
the points of its
two horns. But
Theseus had been
fighting all his life.
With the grace of a
matador, he seemed to
glide to one side, then
whirled around, bring-
ing the sword lashing through the air. The
blade bit into the creature's neck, cutting
through sinew and bone. The Minotaur
shrieked. Its animal head fell away from
its human body. For a moment it stood,

33

gushing blood, its arms flailing. Then it collapsed.

Theseus took one last look at the dead creature, then walked back the way he had come and found the end of the thread. As deadly as it was, the labyrinth was nothing to him. The thread led him straight back to the door and, with a grateful sigh, he let himself out. He was soaked in the Minotaur's blood, bruised and exhausted. But he could not stop yet.

Ariadne had been busy while he was in the labyrinth. She had freed the six Athenian men from their prison and led them out of the palace. Meanwhile, the two soldiers who had come to Knossos disguised as girls had cut the throats of their guards and released the five real maidens. Now they were all waiting on the ship, and as soon as Theseus had managed to find his way out of the palace and down to the harbor, they rowed hastily away, escaping under cover of darkness.

The Minotaur

The End of the Story

Just three knots remain to tie up the loose ends of this tale.

When Minos discovered that the Minotaur was dead, he was so grateful that he forgave Theseus the death of his two guards and the loss of his daughter. The great shame of his life had at last been wiped away and he decided not to ask for further tribute from the Athenians. Never again were young men and women demanded as payment for the death of Androgeus.

Ariadne never received the reward that she had demanded because, sadly, she fell ill on the journey to Athens, and although she was well looked after, she died. Or at least, that is what some versions of the story say. Others have it that Theseus broke his promise and abandoned her on Naxos, the first island he came to. Who is to say which of the two endings is the more likely?

But there was one sad footnote which

nobody disputes.

Theseus was so glad to be returning home safely, he forgot to do what his father had told him and he didn't change the color of the sails. Old Aegeus, watching out for him on the top of the cliff, saw the black sails when the boat was still miles from the coast and, believing his son to have perished, flung himself into the sea. After that, the sea was called the Aegean, a name it still carries to this day.

Theseus was crowned king of Athens. He was a strong if somewhat severe ruler, wiping out virtually all his enemies without a second thought. But his actions paved the way for a secure and flourishing Athens. He was also the first Athenian king to mint money. Should you ever find a Thesean coin,

The Minotaur

you will recognize it easily. For it is stamped
with the head of a bull.

The Great Bell of Peking

Chinese

The Great Bell of Peking

When Peking became the capital of China, it was decreed by the emperor, Yung Lo, that two towers should be built. One would be a lookout tower and would be furnished with a magnificent drum. The other would be an alarm tower and would contain a great bell. This bell would have two purposes. It would be sounded should some enemy be sighted outside the city's walls. But it would also be larger and louder than any other bell in China and as such would be a fitting symbol for the new capital of the country.

Yung Lo therefore approached the most celebrated bell maker in China, a man by the name of Kuan Yu. The emperor explained what was wanted and handed over a purse of gold coins so that Kuan Yu could employ a small army of craftsmen and also buy the necessary amount of metal. Kuan Yu set to work immediately, but it was three months before he was able to announce that the bell was ready.

At once the emperor set out from his

palace in a triumphal procession. Carried in his golden throne and surrounded by courtiers and musicians, he arrived at Kuan Yu's workshop with a great crashing of cymbals and drums. The bell was not actually finished, but the mold in which it was to be cast was complete and the metal for the bell was molten and bubbling.

The emperor took his place and a signal for the last stage of the construction was given. The huge vat of liquid metal was upturned. A silver river ran hissing down the conduits and went swirling into the mold. Then there was a long wait while the metal cooled, until at last the mold could be cracked open and the bell revealed. The emperor and his courtiers leaned forward. The mold was

The Great Bell of Peking

peeled away rather like an eggshell. Kuan Yu went pale. The courtiers gasped. Something had gone wrong! The bell was pitted with holes. The whole thing was useless. Three months' work and a small fortune had just gone down the drain.

Fortunately, Yung Lo was of a forgiving nature. He gave the bell maker another purse of gold and instructed him to start again. Another three months passed, during which time Kuan Yu worked in a fury, checking and rechecking his plans, tending the furnaces and monitoring every phase of the new mold's construction. At last the time came for a second attempt. The emperor was summoned. The workshop was prepared.

As the second silver river trickled along the conduits, nobody spoke. There was another long, tense wait as the mold cooled. Finally, with a trembling hand, Kuan Yu broke it open. This time the shock was so great that he almost fainted. For the bell had cracked into three pieces, one for each month that had gone into its construction. Once again it was useless. Once again the emperor's money had been wasted.

Yung Lo was a patient man. Many emperors would have taken the bell maker's two failures as a personal insult and would have had the poor man put to a horrible death. But he didn't lose his temper. He gave Kuan Yu a third purse of gold, but this time he leaned forward and whispered to him.

"To fail once was understandable," he said. "To fail twice was pardonable. But even I cannot allow you to fail three times."

"I understand, sire," the bell maker quavered.

"One more mistake must cost you your life," the emperor said. "You have three more months to finish the work. Give me my bell or die."

Once more Kuan Yu set to work, but this time it was with a heavy heart. For he had come to believe that the bell was cursed, that he would never be able to finish it correctly, and that, however hard he tried, he would still lose his life. It was in this mood that his daughter found him one evening, sitting by the fire with his head in his hands.

Kuan Yu was a widower. His wife had died of an illness many years before and he lived alone with his daughter, Ko-ai. Now aged sixteen, she was a beautiful girl with soft, almond eyes, long silken lashes, and hair as black as midnight. She was slim and graceful, with a gentle voice that almost sang rather than spoke. As well as looking after the house and cooking for her father, Ko-ai was a skillful poet and a talented painter. Needless to say, Kuan Yu loved his daughter dearly.

Seeing how unhappy her father looked, Ko-ai sat beside him, resting her head in his lap, and asked him what was wrong.

"I have failed my emperor twice," Kuan Yu muttered. "If it happens a third time, I am doomed. And yet . . ." He turned the plans of the third bell over in his hands. "I am afraid," he whispered.

"If only I could help . . ." Ko-ai said.

"There is nothing you can do," Kuan Yu replied. "The casting of the bell is only a few days away. There is nothing more we can do."

The next day, Ko-ai got up early and slipped quietly out of the house. Then she crossed Peking on foot until she came to the house of a famous magician whose name was Kuo Po. As she lifted her hand to knock on the door, it opened by itself and she stepped into a dark, incense-filled passage that led to a circular room where the magician was waiting for her, sitting cross-legged on a rush mat.

"Greetings, Ko-ai," he said.

"You know my name!" she exclaimed.

The magician bowed his bald head. "It is my business to know. I know also the business that brings you here. You have a question. I warn you—don't ask it. The answer may not be to your liking."

"But I must know," Ko-ai said, speaking in a low voice.

"Very well." The magician paused. "The third bell will fail."

Ko-ai fell back, tears starting to her eyes. But then the magician raised a hand.

"The bell will fail," he said, "unless the blood of a young girl is mixed with the molten metal."

"But . . ."

"I warned you not to ask. Now you know. Only the blood of a young girl will save your father from execution. Now leave me!"

The day of the third casting arrived.

Once more the emperor set out from the palace but this time, in addition to the

The Great Bell of Peking

courtiers and musicians, his retinue included
a hooded executioner carrying
an ax. For the third and last
time the cauldron of metal
was heated to
boiling point,

the steam swirling upward, the surface bubbling and spitting. Everyone in the room was sweating . . . and it wasn't just because of the heat.

Then, one second before the signal was given for the cauldron to be upturned, Ko-ai appeared, running along a gantry just below the ceiling.

"Father!" she shouted. "I do this for you!"

Before anyone could stop her, she leaped off the gantry with a terrible scream and dived headfirst into the molten metal. A servant tried to catch her as she fell, but all he caught was her shoe, which came off in his hand.

Kuan Yu cried out and fainted dead away.

His daughter's body hit the surface of the metal and disappeared into it as if through some magical mirror. Her scream was cut off instantly. At once there was a great sizzling and a horrible smell filled the air.

At the same moment, the cauldron, which had already begun to tilt, upturned. The

metal ran out, racing down the conduits and into the mold. But this time it was streaked with red.

Nobody would ever forget the nightmare of that day. Kuan Yu had to be helped to his bedroom where he remained, driven completely mad by what he had seen. From that moment on, whenever he heard the sound of a bell, he would scream and struggle and it would take six strong men to tie him to his bed. The emperor returned to his palace with his stunned courtiers. Never again would his musicians be able to play in tune. Nor, for that matter, would the executioner ever manage to perform another execution, for his nerves had been permanently shattered.

But when the bell had cooled and the mold had been cracked open, it was discovered that, just as the magician had predicted, it was Kuan Yu's greatest triumph. And despite everything, the emperor ordered that it should be hung in the tower as intended.

When the citizens of Peking heard the story of Ko-ai's heroism and saw the bell being carried out of the house by fifty strong men, they became very curious to know what it would sound like. The bell certainly looked peculiar, for the red streaks could still be seen, swirling around in the silver. They watched with interest as it was hauled up and hung in the tower, and when the day came for the first sounding, the streets were so packed that nobody in the city could move. Even the emperor showed up for the first ringing, which was to be at midday exactly.

The sun rose in the sky. At last the moment came.

The bell was struck and indeed the sound was so loud and impressive that the emperor really believed that he had gotten his money's worth. But then the crowd gasped with horror. For the boom of the bell was immediately followed by a ghastly shriek, exactly the same sound that Ko-ai had made as she hit the scalding metal. And even as the scream died away, the word *Hsieh* was heard, whispered inside the bell's echo. *Hsieh* is the Chinese word for shoe—and that was the only part of Ko-ai that had been saved.

Such is the legend of the great bell of Peking. And if you do not believe it, then travel to the city yourself and wait for the bell to be struck. Then you will hear the scream, followed by the whisper, and if anybody asks you what the sound is, you will be able to tell them. It is the sound of a dreadful death.

Romulus
and Remus

Roman

Romulus and Remus

There were once two brothers called Numitor and Amulius.

Numitor was a king, and not a bad one as kings go, ruling over the great city of Alba Longa in northern Italy with a surprising amount of tolerance and generosity. Unfortunately, his younger brother was much less agreeable. It wasn't enough that he was a prince and lived in a palace. Like many powerful men, what he wanted was more power and he would do anything to get it. And so he schemed and whispered and plotted and planned until he had found enough like-minded people to support him, and one day he led an armed attack on the throne, which he seized for his own. King Numitor was taken completely by surprise. He tried to put up a fight but it was too late and suddenly he found himself forced into exile.

Amulius seized all his possessions—and this included his daughter, whose name was Rhea Silvia. The new king couldn't have her killed. She was too popular and too many people would have complained. So instead he forced her to become a vestal virgin (which was quite possibly the next best thing). It meant that she was forbidden to marry or have children—and this was exactly what Amulius wanted. He knew that if Rhea Silvia had any children they might one day grow up to take revenge on him.

But there was one thing Amulius didn't know. Mars, the great god of war, had been keeping his eye on Rhea Silvia, who was young and very pretty. And one night, no longer able to contain himself, he slipped down to earth and surprised Rhea Silvia as she lay sleeping. The result of this—nine months later—was the birth of twins. They were named Romulus and Remus.

King Amulius was furious when he discovered what had happened. Although it was hardly her fault, he had Rhea Silvia thrown into the Tiber River. But his rage didn't end there. With the sort of cruelty that would certainly have alarmed the social services if they had existed at the time, he had the new-born twins locked up in a rope-bound crate and hurled in after her. The mother drowned, but the two boys were more fortunate. A freak current grabbed hold of the box and carried it away, eventually depositing it on the shore just underneath the Palatine Hill.

They still might have starved or suffocated but in another striking turn of events they were discovered by a passing she-wolf, who gnawed through the ropes and found the gurgling and perfectly happy babies inside. The wolf, clearly a remarkable animal, decided to raise Romulus and Remus as if they were her own cubs, suckling them and curling around them to keep them warm at night. They were also fed by woodpeckers, which brought them nuts and fruit and even hunks of meat, and thus they grew up safe and healthy. Since that time, the wolf and the woodpecker have always been the sacred animals of the god Mars.

One day, when the twins were about four years old, they were discovered, living wild in the forest, by a shepherd named Faustulus. He was a kindly soul, with no children of his own, and he decided at once to take them back to his house and look after them. For the first time they wore clothes and ate hot food. Faustulus

Romulus and Remus

taught them how to talk and
his wife taught them how
to read and write.
For ten years they
lived there, treat-
ing Faustulus

as if he were their father.

In those days, shepherds had a hard life, for the country was full of bandits who preyed on them, stealing their livestock or carrying off their food and wine. But by the time Romulus and Remus had reached their teens, they were strong and completely fearless. They were also skilled with both the sword and the staff. And suddenly it was the bandits who found themselves under attack.

Romulus and Remus became so skillful in robbing the robbers that they soon gained a reputation that spread throughout the whole country. Everywhere they went, the shepherds were pleased to see them and even the sheep seemed glad to have them around. It was inevitable, though, that their luck would turn and one day they found themselves taken by surprise, surrounded by a gang of thirty snarling bandits led by a brute by the name of Josephus.

Josephus was immensely fat, with a beard

Romulus and Remus

that framed his face like brown tassels on a pink cushion. Whenever his men stole a sheep he would eat at least half of it, and sometimes he wouldn't even wait until the poor thing was dead. Anyway, he was the man in charge of the ambush and although Romulus and Remus fought bravely, it was obvious that they were hopelessly outnumbered. Even so, they managed to kill at least twenty of the enemy before their swords finally broke. Romulus managed to get away, but Remus was captured and brought before the bandit king.

"Shall we kill him, my lord?" the bandits cried. Josephus was a peasant, not a lord, but that was the name he liked to be called.

"No." Josephus thought for a moment, not an activity that came easily to him. He was strong and he was crooked but he wasn't particularly bright. "Let's carry him to a local landowner," he suggested. "That way he'll get the blame for all our crimes and we'll be in the clear."

If the bandits had considered this proposition, they would have seen that there wasn't much logic to it, but since when have bandits ever been logical? They were good at killing people and stealing things but not much else. This was why they had become bandits. And now they did as they were told, tying Remus up with so much rope that he couldn't move and then carrying him on their shoulders into the nearest town.

Romulus and Remus

In this way, they brought him before the local landowner, an elderly man who lived on his own, surrounded by books and musical instruments. They tried to explain that this was a villain they had caught in the woods and that he was responsible for all the crimes in the area—but despite everything he heard, the old man refused to believe them. First of all, the bandits didn't exactly make reliable witnesses, shouting over each other to make themselves heard and stabbing anyone who interrupted them. But there was also something about the young man's bearing. He didn't look like a criminal. In fact he looked almost noble.

He asked Remus to talk about himself, and as Remus told his story, he was surprised to see tears spring from the old man's eyes. For it turned out that the old man was none other than Numitor, the king who had been deposed by his younger brother. Numitor had of course heard what had happened to his poor daughter, Rhea Silvia. He had also heard rumors that she had given birth before she died, and it had to be said that this young man looked very much like her. In any event, he was more than happy to put two and two together and to agree without any doubt that Remus must be his grandson.

Josephus and the surviving bandits were immediately arrested. A search party was sent into the woods to find Romulus, and that night the three of them—Numitor, Romulus, and Remus—dined together, reunited at last as a family.

A few weeks later, Numitor returned to Alba Longa with his two grandsons riding beside him and a sizable army following behind. King Amulius was completely un-prepared. He had spent the past fourteen years drinking wine and chasing the palace maidservants, and by the time he learned that there was an army at the door, it was already too late. He was shot down in a hail of arrows and nobody was sorry to see the end of him. That same day, Numitor was returned to the throne.

With Numitor once again in power, you might have thought that all would have ended happily for Romulus and Remus, but sadly this was not the case.

The two brothers had decided that they wanted a city of their own and, taking their leave of Numitor, they returned to the Palatine where they had been washed up all those years ago. But now the jealousy which began the story, and which had always run in the family's blood, began to surface.

"We shall build a great city," Remus said. "And I shall be king."

"Forgive me," Romulus countered. "Surely I ought to be king of our new city."

"Why should you be king?" Remus asked.

"Well, it was my idea to build the city in the first place."

"Hold on a minute, my dear brother," Remus said, turning a little red. "If I hadn't been carried off by Josephus, none of this

would ever have happened."

"Being captured by an overweight bandit is nothing to be proud of," Romulus countered, turning red himself. "It was my idea and I shall be king of the new city and it will be called Rome, after me."

"I shall be king," Remus cried. "And it shall be called Reme, after me."

"Rome!"

"Reme!"

There seemed to be no way to resolve the argument. For, being twins, they couldn't even say who was the older—which might have been one way to decide the matter. But at the same time, they were unwilling to fight each other. They had been through too much together for that.

In the end, they decided to let the gods sort it out. Romulus climbed the Palatine Hill, while Remus climbed the nearby Aventine.* They didn't have to wait long for the omen.

---

* Even today, if you visit Rome, you will find that there's still a rivalry between those two areas of the city. This footnote gives away the end of the story but you'd probably guessed it anyway.

Almost at once the clouds folded back and six great vultures flew down to the Aventine and began to circle around Remus.

"There you are!" Remus shouted triumphantly. "The city will be Reme and I will be king. The gods have decided it."

"No!" Romulus shouted back. "The gods are on my side. The city will be Rome and I will rule. Look!"

Remus looked up, the color draining out of his face as twelve more vultures soared out of the sky to flap around his brother. Romulus had twice as many birds. Remus had lost.

Remus took his defeat with bad grace, and after that there was never any love between him and his brother. In fact even after the new city had been constructed, he took every opportunity to taunt Romulus about it, saying that the streets were too narrow and the walls too high, that there were too many temples and not enough shops. Things finally came to a head when Romulus dug out the long trench that marked the city's boundaries and Remus jumped over it, laughing, as if to say that Rome could be captured just as easily. For Romulus, this was the last straw. He drew his sword. It flashed through the air. And before he knew what he had done, his brother lay at his feet in a spreading pool of blood.

In this way was the city of Rome founded —in blood. And perhaps it was the reason why so much blood would flow through its streets in the next two thousand years.

But that is not the matter of myth or of legend. That is a matter of history.

Geriguiaguiatugo

Bororo Indian

Geriguiaguiatugo

The Bororo Indians of South America tell a strange story about a young man with the difficult name of Geriguiaguiatugo. Before I get started, it might be worth mentioning a few things.

1. These myths and legends, told by primitive people, often have no logic. They belong to a world that was utterly different from ours.
2. They can be extremely violent.
3. Every version is slightly different. The Bororo Indians had an oral tradition, passing the stories from generation to generation.
4. I have drawn together what versions I could find but have added very little of my own.

In any event, the story starts with Geriguiaguiatugo violently attacking his mother in a forest. I have no idea what the poor woman had done to deserve this but that's how it usually begins.

Anyway, with his mother lying, brutally

beaten, on the forest floor, Geriguiaguiatugo returned to his village and went on living as if nothing had happened. His father, however, was suspicious. It was nothing he could put his finger on—the bruises on his son's knuckles or the enormous bloodstains on his loincloth, perhaps—but he somehow felt certain that the boy was responsible for his wife's terrible injuries.

He therefore decided to take revenge and sent Geriguiaguiatugo on a number of missions, each one more dangerous than the last. For example, he ordered his son to remove a sacred rattle from the Lake of Souls. This lake was a nightmare place where dead men's hands would break through the black surface of the water to drag unsuspecting travelers down to a freezing death. But Geriguiaguiatugo survived. Guided by a hummingbird, he sailed right across, snatched up the sacred rattle, and brought it back to the village, whistling so cheerfully that he might have come back from a day's fishing.

Geriguiaguiatugo

Although he tried not to show it, the father was furious that his son had returned unhurt and immediately gave him a second task—and this time the two of them set off together. They were going in search of a rare parrot, the father explained, but it could only be found at the top of a cliff some distance away. Geriguiaguiatugo had no reason to doubt this story. He had no idea there was anything wrong.

The cliff, when they reached it, however, was fantastically high. Standing at the bottom with his head tilted back, Geriguiaguiatugo couldn't see where the sheer rock face ended and the sky began. It seemed to go on forever.

"How will we ever get to the top?" he asked.

His father drove an iron nail into the cliff, missing his son's head by inches. "We'll climb," he growled.

And that was what they did. It was slow, exhausting work. There were hardly any footholds and the few ledges were tiny and treacherous. Even Geriguiaguiatugo, who was physically fit and afraid of nothing, found it hard going. One moment his foot would be firmly fixed against the rock face. The next, his stomach would lurch and he would scrabble madly for support, with the stone crumbling beneath his feet. Soon the ground was far, far below. Looking down, Geriguiaguiatugo could see trees that were now no bigger than heliconia.* Swearing

---

* Bright flowers found in the rainforest.

under his breath, he concen-
trated on searching for a
way to conquer the next six
inches of the cliff.

His father was climb-
ing directly beneath him.
At one stage there wasn't
a single foothold in sight
and Geriguiaguiatugo had to
hammer in a whole staircase
of nails that stretched for about
thirty feet. That was when his
father struck. Using his bare
hands, he pulled out all the
nails, cut the rope that
connected him to his son,
and climbed back down
the way he had come.
When he turned around,
Geriguiaguiatugo found
himself stranded.

"You swine!" he shouted.
"You can't leave me here!"

81

"Yes I can!" came back the cheery reply.

"Come back! What about the mission? What about the parrot? What about me?"

But the father just laughed.

Soon he had disappeared altogether and Geriguiaguiatugo was forced to take stock of his situation. It was not a pleasant one. He was halfway up a cliff. His hands were raw and bleeding after all his effort. Night was drawing in. Although he still had the hammer and the bag of nails, it was physically impossible to knock in a fresh staircase underneath his feet. And yet without the staircase, there was certainly no way down. The cliff face was too smooth, too dangerous.

That only left up.

He began to climb. He climbed until every muscle in his body screamed at him and the tears ran down his cheeks.

"What did I do to deserve this?" he moaned (forgetting, for the moment, his hospitalized mother). "How could my father do this to me? Well, it's nothing compared with what I'll do to the old fool when I catch up with him . . ."

One slip, and the story would have ended then and there. But somehow Geriguiaguiatugo managed to reach the top. His troubles, however, were far from over. As his father had known from the very start, the cliff simply led to a small plateau and there was nothing there: no plants, no water, no birds . . . not so much as a rare parrot's feather. He had reached the top but it seemed that all that awaited him was a slow death by starvation.

By now the sun had gone down and a pale moon hung in the sky. Geriguiaguiatugo was surprised to discover that he was no longer alone. A whole colony of lizards inhabited the arid rocks at the top of the cliff, and now that the heat of the day was over, they were coming out to stretch themselves in the dust.

But at least that was good news. For the

Bororo Indians, lizard was something of a delicacy. They frequently ate it fried in a little chicken fat and flavored with herbs. It was just as good caught fresh and alive, crunched raw between the teeth. In a matter of seconds, Geriguiaguiatugo had snatched up a couple of fat specimens, stunning them with his hammer. He ate them immediately. Then he caught half a dozen more and hung them on a string around his waist.

The next day, when he woke up, the sun was hotter than ever. It was far too hot even to think about finding a way off the plateau, so he just sat there, amusing himself by dreaming up ever more painful things to do to his father when he got back to the village. Around midday, he began to notice an unpleasant smell. By the end of the afternoon, the smell had become nauseating. He got up and walked over to the other side of the plateau. The smell followed him. An hour later it had become so bad that he reeled, staggered, and finally lost consciousness.

The dead lizards were to blame. Hanging around his waist in the hot sun, the corpses had all started to rot—and now their stench attracted a passing flock of vultures. The ghastly birds with their bald heads, ragged green feathers, and twisting necks liked their meat best when it was spoiled.

As one they landed on the unconscious body of Geriguiaguiatugo and began to tear into the rotten flesh with their beaks and talons. And they were so hungry that they didn't stop with the lizards. They also ate Geriguiaguiatugo's buttocks, tearing the flesh off and swallowing that too.

Geriguiaguiatugo woke up some time later and he was so relieved to find that the smell had gone that he didn't even notice his hideous mutilation. A short distance away, the vultures watched as he explored the edge of the cliff, searching for a way down.

"We owe the boy a favor," one of them said. "Maybe we should take him down to the bottom."

Several of the vultures laughed, hearing this. After all, it was his bottom they had just devoured . . . a fairly feeble joke, but then vultures have an underdeveloped sense of humor.

"If we leave him here, he's got precious little future ahead of him," the vulture insisted.

"He's got precious little behind him too," another vulture observed.

So the birds flew back to Geriguiaguiatugo and, hooking their claws into his shirt, lifted him clear off the ground and carried him all the way to the foot of the cliff.

Geriguiaguiatugo was completely astonished by this stroke of good fortune and began the journey back to the village, pausing only to pluck some fruit from a tree, for he was hungry again. It was then that he discovered what had happened to him. For, having no bottom, the fruit literally went straight through him. But he wasn't upset. He remembered how his grandmother had used to make him eat his mashed potatoes when he was a little boy—forming them into shapes on his plate. And so he dug up some sweet potatoes, boiled and mashed them, and finally formed them into a new pair of buttocks which he fitted neatly into place.

Feeling much more complete, he made his way back to his village. The journey took him several weeks but, even so, the villagers were still celebrating his supposed death when he got back. They immediately tried to pretend that they were actually mourning for him but Geriguiaguiatugo wasn't fooled. Nor was he impressed when his father crawled forward to greet him.

"Hello, son," the father said, trying to fix a smile to his lips even as the blood drained from his face.

"Hello, father," Geriguiaguiatugo replied. "Been doing any rock climbing lately?"

"Well . . ." The old man blushed. "I did try to get back to you. Honest! But . . ."

"But?"

"But . . ."

"I'll butt you, you old buffoon!"

And with those words, Geriguiaguiatugo magically transformed himself into a stag and charged at his father, butting him to the ground. The villagers groaned, but he wasn't finished yet. He hooked his horns into his father's stomach and then shot the old man into the air with one flick of his neck. Three times he did it. The first time, the father landed in a clump of thistles. The second time he hit a wasp's nest. And the third time he splashed into a nearby river, where he

was immediately torn into a million pieces by a pack of ravenous piranhas.

After that, Geriguiaguiatugo ruled over the village. And I can only finish by saying that they all lived horribly ever after.

Given to the Sun

Inca

"Why do we Incas worship the Sun?" the boy asked.

"Have you not been taught that at school?" the Inca priest demanded crossly.

"I am too young to have gone to school," the boy replied.

The priest softened. "Very well," he said. "I will tell you the story of how the Sun came into the land . . ."

"There was a time, long ago, when the whole land was covered in darkness. It was a cruel and desolate wilderness, with rocky mountains stretching into the north and great cliffs plunging down in the south. The people knew nothing then. They were hardly better than beasts, going naked in the fields, without shame. They had neither houses nor villages but lived in caves, huddling together for warmth, unable even to light a fire. They fed on wild fruit and whatever animals they could catch—wild rats and foxes—tearing at the meat with their teeth and swallowing it raw. When times were particularly hard,

they ate grass or the roots of weeds and wild plants and sometimes (horrible to say) they might even feast on human flesh.

"Then came Inti—for that is the name we have given to the Sun, a name that only a true Inca may utter—and his light lit the world and showed up the wretched state of the people. And because the Sun was kind, he was ashamed for them. So he decided to send one of his sons down from heaven to earth. This son of the Sun would show men and women how to till the soil, how to sow seed, to raise cattle, to bring in the fruits of the harvest. He would also teach them to worship the Sun as their god, for without light and warmth they could be no better than animals."

"What was the name of the son of the Sun?" the boy asked.

"His name was Manco Capac," the priest said. "And with him came Occlo Huaco. She was the daughter of the Moon."

"Were the Sun and the Moon friends?"

"They were married to each other," the priest explained. "So the two children were brother and sister."

"Manco Capac and Occlo Huaco were set down on two islands in Lake Titicaca, which is the highest lake in the world. Even to this day they are known as the Islands of the Sun and the Moon. Then they walked across the lake, the water sparkling like diamonds at their feet, until at last they stepped onto dry land and began their work.

"Before they had left heaven, the Sun had given them a rod of gold. It was about as thick as two fingers and a little shorter than a man's arm.

" 'Go where you will,' he had told them. 'But whenever you stop to sleep or to eat, try pushing this rod into the earth. If it won't go in, or only goes in a little way, keep moving. But when you reach a spot where, with a single thrust, the rod disappears completely, you will know that you are in a place that is sacred to me. And that is where you must stay. For you will be at the site of what will become a great city, full of palaces and temples. And that city will be the center of my empire, an empire such as has never been seen before in the world.' "

"Manco Capac and Occlo Huaco left Lake Titicaca and began walking toward the north. Every day, they tried to push their rod of gold into the earth, but without success. This went on for many weeks until at last they came to the valley of Cuzco, which was then nothing more than a wild, mountainous desert. When they tried their rod here, it disappeared completely into the ground and so they knew they had reached the place where the Inca empire was to be founded.

"The two of them then went their separate ways, talking to any savages they happened to meet, explaining why they were there. The savages, of course, were hugely impressed. For the strangers were dressed in beautiful clothes. Gold discs hung from their ears. Their hair was short and tidy and their bodies were clean. There had never been two people like them and soon thousands of men and women had come to the valley of Cuzco to see the two visitors and to hear what they had to say.

"That was when Manco Capac began building the city that his father had demanded.

At the same time, he and his sister taught the people everything they needed to know if they were to be properly civilized."

"Was the city the same city that we are in now?" the boy asked.

"Yes," the priest said. "It was called Cuzco. And it was divided into two halves. Upper Cuzco was built by our king. Lower Cuzco was built by the queen."

"Why were there two halves?"

"It was built like the human body, with a

101

right side and a left side. All our cities have been built the same way. But the Sun is rising, boy. I'm afraid we must very soon finish the story . . ."

"In only a short time, the savages were savage no more. They lived in brick houses and wore real clothing. Manco Capac had taught the men how to cultivate the fields while his sister had taught the women how to spin and weave. There was even an army in Cuzco with bows and arrows and spears, ready to fight those people who still remained in the wild. But gradually the empire spread and Manco Capac became the first Inca, which is to say the first king of the Inca people.

"Always since then, the Incas have worshiped the Sun. For every Inca king who reigns is a descendant of Manco Capac, which means that he is also a descendant of the Sun. The Sun gives light and warmth and makes the crops grow. The Sun sent his own son into the world so that the people

would no longer behave like animals. Great
temples have been built
to honor the Sun, reflect-
ing his rays in sheets of
beaten gold.

"And on Inti Raymi—
which is the summer
solstice, the day when
the Sun is at the
furthest extreme
of his journey
south—there
is a festival
with music
and dancing
and feasting.
On that day,
sacrifices are
made. Llamas
have their throats
cut before being
put on the fire.
The smoke

rises into the air and in this way they are given to the Sun. And if there is a special event to be celebrated, a great victory for example, then it is not an animal but a child that must die."

"And I am to be given to the Sun," the boy whispered.

"That is your honor, my child," the priest said.

The sun had risen above the horizon now. The priest forced the boy back against the sacrificial stone, then thrust the ceremonial knife deep into his heart. A fire was lit. And soon the smoke was curling upward, up into the brilliant sky.

The Ugly Wife

Celtic

The Ugly Wife

This is a tale of King Arthur, the legendary king of Britain who ruled over the famous Knights of the Round Table. It is also about Sir Gawain, the nephew of King Arthur and the noblest of those who sat at the Round Table. It begins (as so many of these tales do) with a damsel in distress.

She came while the court was in Carlisle. Her hair was bedraggled, her clothes torn, and her eyes wild with grief.

"Help me, King Arthur!" she cried. "My husband has been stolen from me and enslaved by the wicked knight of Tarn Wathelyne. Though I fought him—you can see that my clothes are torn and I'm covered with bruises—there was nothing I could do. My husband is gone! And so I turn to you, great king. Give him back to me. Slay the knight of Tarn Wathelyne."

When King Arthur heard this, he was shocked but quietly pleased. The sight of the poor woman genuinely moved him, but at

the same time he secretly
loved adventure and couldn't
help looking forward to this new chal-
lenge. The very same day he set out on his
horse. He went alone, armed only with a
spear and with Excalibur, his magic sword,
and as he went he whistled. For King Arthur
had never known fear—or if he had, he had
never shown it.

111

But this time something very strange happened. As he rode further and further into a wood (which became steadily darker and darker), the whistle died on his lips. He passed a lake as black as blood on a moonless night and his whole body shivered. All the trees had lost their leaves. Their branches writhed like snakes in the wind and ragged crows hung above them, screeching at each other as if sharing unpleasant secrets. Despite himself, King Arthur was shivering and he knew it wasn't just because of the cold.

At last he saw the knight's castle. It was vast, wider at the top than at the bottom, with two dark windows high up and a solid black portcullis below. From a distance, it resembled an enormous human skull. King Arthur forced himself on, guiding his horse toward the drawbridge. But when the portcullis opened with a loud metallic creaking and the knight of Tarn Wathelyne rode out, the last of his courage left him.

With a groan, Arthur fell to the ground, almost fainting with fear.

The knight, invisible in his black armor, dismounted from his horse and walked over to where Arthur knelt. The king could not find the strength to look up. He heard the crunch of footsteps on gravel and the clink of armor. Then came the sound of metal scraping against metal as the knight drew out his sword. There was a minute's silence that seemed to drag on for an hour. Finally came a voice as cold as death itself.

"So this is the great King Arthur!" it whispered. "Tell me—Your Majesty—why should I not lop off your head while you grovel before me?"

"You . . . are . . . the . . . devil!" King Arthur gasped.

"No!" The knight laughed. "My name is Gromer Somer Joure and I am the servant of Queen Morgana le Fay, your sworn enemy. But see—the lady is here, with me."

With an effort, King Arthur raised his

head and there, beside the knight, was the woman who had sent him on the quest in the first place. But now she was smiling malevolently at him. Morgana had magically disguised herself, and even in his fear King Arthur trembled with anger at how easily he had been deceived.

"Have pity on me!" he cried.

"Killing you now would be too easy," the knight replied. "So instead I will send you on a quest. Swear to me that you will return here, on your own, exactly one year from now. But when you come back, you must answer me this question: What is it that women want most in the world? If you can give me the correct answer, I will spare your miserable life. But if you are wrong, then, King Arthur, you will die. You will die slowly—and your bones will decorate my castle walls."

The black knight laughed, then took Morgana's hand. The two of them moved away. The portcullis came crashing down and King Arthur was left alone.

The Answer

"It was sorcery, my lord," Sir Gawain cried when he heard this story. "It was black magic. That was what caused your fear. That's what made you cry out for mercy. By your leave, I will ride out to the castle and . . ."

"No, my dear Gawain." King Arthur

stopped him. "I have been sent on a quest. I am honor-bound. What is it that women most desire in this world? I have a year to find out."

"Then I will come with you," Gawain said. "Maybe together we'll have more luck."

The next day they left Carlisle and rode out across the country, stopping every woman they met in an attempt to find the solution to the knight's riddle. The trouble was, nobody they met could agree.

Some said that women most desired jewels and fine clothes. Others insisted that a good husband and loving children were more important. Luxury, loyalty, immortality, independence . . . these were just some of the answers they were given. There was one old lunatic who insisted that all women really wanted was strawberry jam. The answers ranged from the bizarre to the banal—but not one of them seemed entirely convincing.

Time passed quickly. A week turned into

a month. Another month passed, then two, then six . . . Soon King Arthur and Sir Gawain found themselves on the way back to the enchanted castle. They had a whole catalog of answers in their saddlebags, but both knew in their hearts that they had failed.

It was on the day before they were to part company, perhaps forever, that they met an old woman. They had stopped in a clearing to rest their horses when Gawain saw her sitting beside a stream, reading a book. His first thought was that she was beautifully dressed, for she wore the finest materials and her whole body was covered with jewels. Then she turned her head and he realized that she was without doubt the ugliest woman he had ever seen.

She really was quite remarkable. Her two lips, like those of a giant ape, met several inches in front of her nose and when she smiled, her teeth stuck out, yellow and uneven. Her skin was the color and the texture of rice pudding and her hair, thin

and wiry, sprouted out of her head without
any obvious color or shape. Her nose had
been pushed into her face until it had almost
disappeared and she had such a bad squint
that she seemed to be trying to look up her
own nostrils. Finally, she was horrendously
fat—so fat, in fact, that her hands and feet
appeared to sprout out of her body without
the benefit of arms and legs.

But she was a woman and, seeing her,
King Arthur decided to have one last crack
at the question. He approached her, bowing
courteously, but before he could speak, she
addressed him in a weird, cackling voice.

"I know the question you wish to ask," she screeched, "and I also know the answer. But I will give it to you on one condition only."

"And what would that be?" King Arthur demanded.

The horrible woman grinned at Gawain and ran a wet tongue over her lips.

"That knight . . ." she said, giggling. "He is young and handsome. What lovely fair hair! What delicate blue eyes! I'd like to have him as my husband. That is my condition! If you will give him to me in marriage, I will save your life."

At this, Gawain went pale. He was indeed young and good-looking. All his friends expected him to come home one day with a beautiful wife. What would they say if he were coupled with this monster . . . ?

But even as these thoughts rushed into his mind, second, nobler thoughts prevailed. He had a duty—to his uncle, and to the king.

"My lord," he said. "If this woman can save your life . . ."

"I can! I can!" the woman crooned.

". . . then I will gladly marry her."

"My dear nephew," King Arthur cried. "You are generous and you are noble. But I can't let you . . ."

"You can't stop me," Gawain replied. He fell onto one knee. "Lady," he exclaimed. "I pledge you my word as a Knight of the Round Table that I will marry you if you can save the king. Tell him what it is that women most desire—and what you desire you will have."

And so it was that the next morning King Arthur rode—alone, as he had promised—to the castle of Tarn Wathelyne. Once again the sense of evil surrounded him like a great darkness, but this time he was able to ride forward with confidence, as though the

answer he carried were a blazing beacon. For a second time the great portcullis ground open and the black knight rode out, his sword already unsheathed.

"So you've returned, great king!" he growled. "I wondered if you'd even be brave enough." His hand reached for his sword. "Tell me the answer to my question. What is it that women most desire in this world?"

King Arthur replied boldly and clearly, repeating what the ugly woman had said to him. "It is this," he said. "All women ask for is that, like men, they should be able to control their own bodies and that they should be allowed to make decisions for themselves."

For a moment the black knight was silent. Then he dropped his sword and, to Arthur's astonishment, fell to his knees.

"You have answered correctly, sire," he said, "and by doing so you have broken the spell that the evil witch Morgana le Fay had cast over me. She forced me to send you on your quest. I was her unwilling slave.

The Ugly Wife

But now that her magic is ended, I beg you, sire, let me come and serve you at the Round Table. For beneath this foul black armor I am a good man and will prove myself worthy of you."

"You are welcome," King Arthur said, and as he spoke the dread castle of Tarn Wathelyne cracked and crumbled and suddenly there was a rushing wind as the bricks and ironwork began to collapse. Then the sunlight broke through the clouds.

The castle shattered, the ground beneath it heaving as if glad to be rid of it. A moment later it had vanished, and once again the birds were singing.

"Let us ride together," King Arthur said, and so it was that they turned back to the court. But although the adventure had ended well for him, his heart was heavy. He had a wedding to attend, a nephew to see married. He would have given his kingdom for it to be otherwise.

The Wedding

The marriage of Sir Gawain was an event that nobody would ever forget. The ugly woman giggled during the service and ate so grotesquely at the feast afterward that almost as much food went down her dress as into her mouth. She sat with her legs apart and her elbows on the table and deliberately forgot everyone's names.

Of course, this being the age of chivalry,

the other wedding guests forced themselves to be scrupulously polite. When Sir Gawain's new wife got drunk and fell over, they rushed forward to help her up as if she had merely stumbled. When she made coarse and unpleasant jokes, they laughed and applauded. And they all congratulated Sir Gawain on his good fortune with as much sincerity as they could muster.

Poor Gawain was the politest of all of them. Not once did he let on that he had married the ghastly woman because he had been forced to. He called her "my lady" and held her arm on the way to the table. When she emptied (or knocked over) her wine goblet, he refilled it for her. And although he was rather silent and sometimes looked as if he was about to faint, he continued to pretend that nothing was wrong.

But at the end of the evening, when he found himself alone in the bedchamber with his ugly wife and saw her powdering her nose and all three of her chins, it all proved too much for him. He clutched his sword. He clutched his hair. Then he burst into tears.

"What is it, my dear?" the lady asked. "What has so upset you on your wedding night?"

"Lady," Gawain replied, "I cannot conceal my thoughts from you. You forced me to become your husband. In truth, I would rather have not."

"And why is that?" the lady demanded.

"I cannot say."

"Tell me!"

"Very well." Gawain took a deep breath. "I do not want to offend you, my lady, but you are old and ugly and evidently of low birth.

Forgive me. I speak only what I feel."

"But what's so wrong?" the woman gurgled. "With age come wisdom and discretion. Are these not good things for a wife to possess? Maybe I am ugly. But if so, you will never have to worry about rivals while you are married to me. Other men might live in fear that someone will run off with their wives. But not you. Finally, you accuse me of being of low birth. Are you really such a snob, Gawain? Do you think that nobility comes just because you are born into a good family? Surely it depends on the character of a person! Can you not teach me to be noble like you?"

Gawain thought for a moment. Despite his innermost feelings, he could not help but agree that the old woman had a point. At the same time, he felt ashamed. Whatever he thought of her, she had saved the life of his uncle. He had behaved badly toward her. He had not behaved like a Knight of the Round Table.

"My lady," he said. "You are right in everything you say. I have spoken discourteously toward you and I apologize."

"Then come to bed," she said. But even as she spoke, Gawain detected something different in her voice and when he turned around he saw to his amazement that she had changed. It was no fat and ugly woman that lay on his bed but a young, beautiful girl with fair skin and soft, green eyes.

"Gawain," she said, smiling at him. "Let me explain. Gromer Somer Joure, or the black knight as you knew him, is my brother. Both of us were enslaved by the wicked Queen Morgana le Fay. I helped the king release my brother from her spell, but only the kindness and understanding of a noble spirit could save me from my horrible enchantment. That is what you have given me, dear Gawain, and now, at last, you see me as I really am. I am your wife—if you will have me. But this time the choice is really yours."

Gawain gazed at her, speechless. Then he

took her hand in his own and held it close to his cheek.

The next morning the court was astounded to see what had happened, and the king ordered a second wedding feast so that this time everyone could really enjoy themselves without having to pretend. Gawain and his lady lived happily together for many years and, although nobody ever told the story when either of them was present (for fear of embarrassing them), on many a winter's night the knights and their pages would gather around the crackling fire to hear once again the strange tale of the ugly wife.

Ten Awesome Weapons of Myth and Legend

. . . but I've made one of them up. Can you spot the intruder?

Caladbolg

The sword of Fergus mac Roich, a hero from Irish mythology. Caladbolg (its name means "hard lightning") was said to create rainbows when it was swung—and it was so powerful that it could cut the tops off mountains.

Ruyi Jingu Bang

This was a magical staff that belonged to Sun Wukong, the Monkey King of Chinese legend. It was heavier than a Tyrannosaurus Rex (about 7.5 tons), but on command it could shrink to the size of a needle.

Kusanagi

Discovered in the belly of an eight-headed monster, this legendary Japanese sword could control the direction of the wind when swung.

The Poison Arrows
of Heracles (Hercules)

A wound from one of these arrows, dipped in the poisonous blood of the nine-headed Lernean Hydra, meant a fast and very painful death.

Excalibur

Without a doubt the most famous sword in England, Excalibur was famously drawn out of a stone by the young Arthur before he became king and stayed with him all his life.

Zeus's thunderbolt

The thunderbolt was the weapon of Zeus, king of the gods in Greek mythology. It was given to him by the one-eyed giant known as Cyclops and he would throw it like a spear

Gniyl Mion

In Celtic mythology, this was the huge cannon that protected the palace of Camulos, the god of war. Each cannonball was the size of a world and it was said that if it ever fired, the universe would end.

Gáe Bulg

A deadly spear from Irish mythology, said to be made from the bone of a sea monster. The spear would enter the victim like a javelin and then split into many barbs that would pierce every part of his body, invariably proving fatal.

Poseidon's trident

A three-pronged spear used by Poseidon, the god of the sea. When he was angry, Poseidon could create earthquakes and tsunamis simply by banging his trident on the ground.

Mjöllnir—the hammer of Thor

Mjöllnir's name means "crusher" and it was the weapon of Thor, the god of thunder in Norse mythology. It never missed its mark when it was thrown, and it could level a whole mountain with a single blow.

The fake weapon is Cniyl Mion (although there really was a god of war called Camulos). There was a clue. *Cniyl Mion* is "No—I'm lying" backward.